I0557251

BURNING TONGUE

Prisoner's Cinema

ALR026

Published by

Aqualamb

BUNING TONGUE
Wilson Flores: Drums
Michael Beaujean: Guitar
Mark Sergenian: Bass
Chris Marotta: Vocals

ALBUM CREDITS
Recorded at Chapel Black Studios, Brooklyn
Engineered and Produced by Wilson Flores
Mastered by Brad Boatright at Audiosiege Media

Additional vocals on "No Honest Man" by David Castillo
Additional vocals on "Throne of Salt" by Chuck Berrett
All Songs ©Burning Tongue 2021

BOOK CREDITS
Cover art: Chris Marotta & "BT" Symbol by John Sokorai
Book design: Sebas Ribas
Band photos: Nathaniel Shannon

First Printing: Edition of 500
ISBN: 979-8-9857365-0-2

Public domain writings and text from: John Martin's Illustrations of Paradise Lost (1827), Compendium Of Demonology and
Magic (ca. 1775), The Spirit Photographs of William Hope, Thomas
Wright's An Original, Theory or New Hypothesis of the Universe
(1750), The Beast of Gévaudan (1764–1767), The Art of Dreams
(Thomas Browne, On Dreams, Elizabeth Bisland, Dreams and
their Mysteries), Worlds Without End By Philip Ball.

All Illustrations © by their respective authors and artists.
All Rights Reserved

aqualamb.org

Aqualamb

Prisoner's Cinema

The music for *Prisoner's Cinema*
can be downloaded via the link below:

aqualamb.org/026

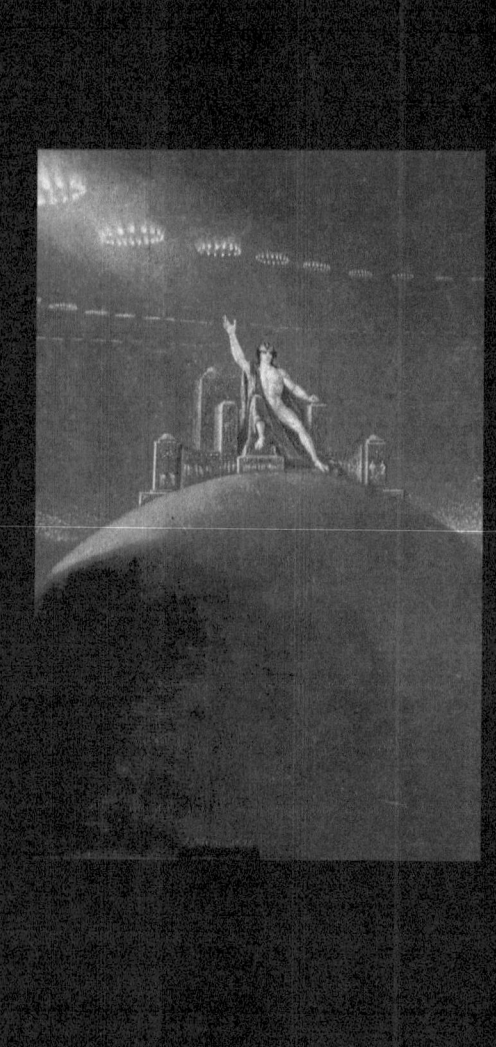

Paradise *lost*

COLLECTION I

John Martin's Illustrations

1867

Paradise Lost (1667) tells the oldest story in the book. Blind as Homer and permanently exiled from political life after the Restoration of 1660, John Milton dictated an epic of the series of falls — of the angels, of Adam and Eve, of human language — that led to the corrupt and warlike world in which he lived. His declared intention was to "assert eternal providence / And justify the ways of God to men." But as every reader of Paradise Lost can attest, Lucifer and the other fallen angels come out far more interesting than God, a peculiarity that prompted William Blake to claim that Milton was "of the Devil's party without knowing it".

Illustrators of Paradise Lost have often drawn more from the poem's infernal depths than its heavenly heights. Blake's wild watercolors (painted in about 1807) delight in depicting the muscular immensity of Satan, spying on Adam and Eve and coaxing them to sin. Gustave Doré's etchings (circa 1866) bask in the possibilities of inky darkness and pay special attention to the angels' wings, which are swan-like as long as they are allied with heaven but turn bat-like the moment they fall. In 1824, the English artist John Martin (1789–1854) was commissioned to offer up his own interpretation — producing a set of images that were originally sold to subscribers and then, in 1827, used to adorn a large two-volume edition of the poem. His mezzotint engravings, too, emphasize the devil and the darkness. Like Blake, he portrays the bodies of God, the angels, Adam and Eve as classically beautiful; like Doré, he uses light and shadow to point up the drama inherent in Milton's scenes. But Martin, a radical romantic at heart, is especially excited by the drama of the scenery — whether the caverns and crags of hell or the English oaks and cumulonimbus clouds of Eden.

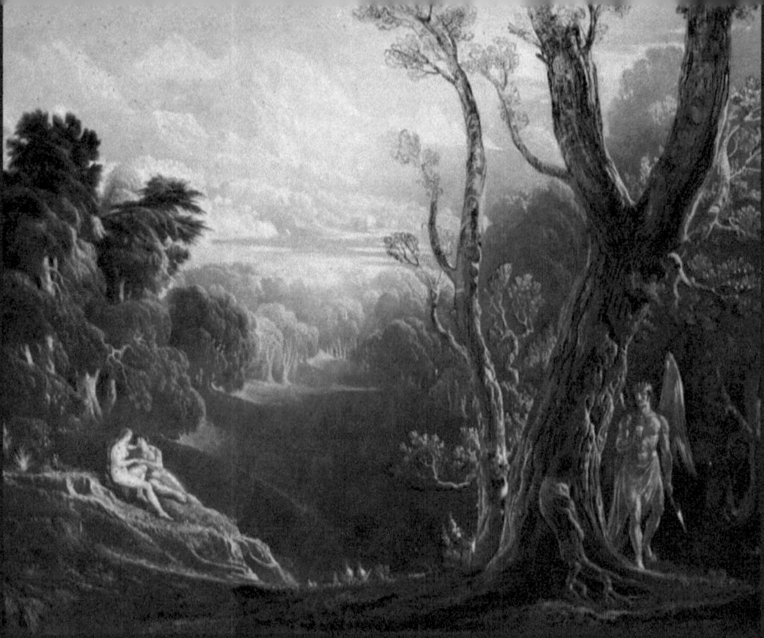

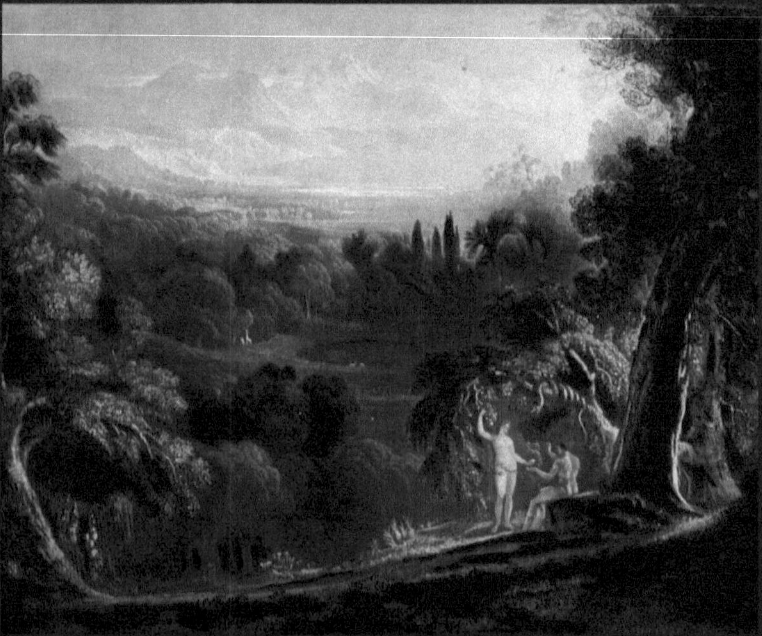

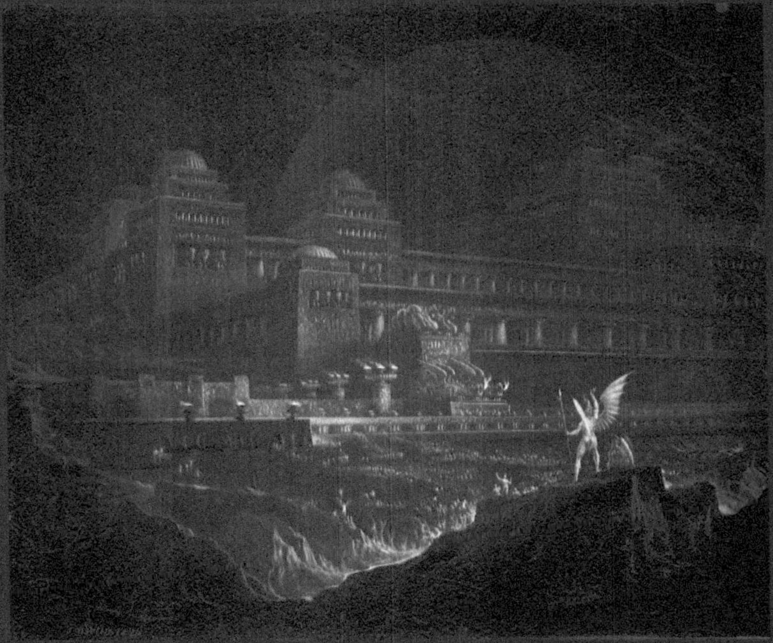

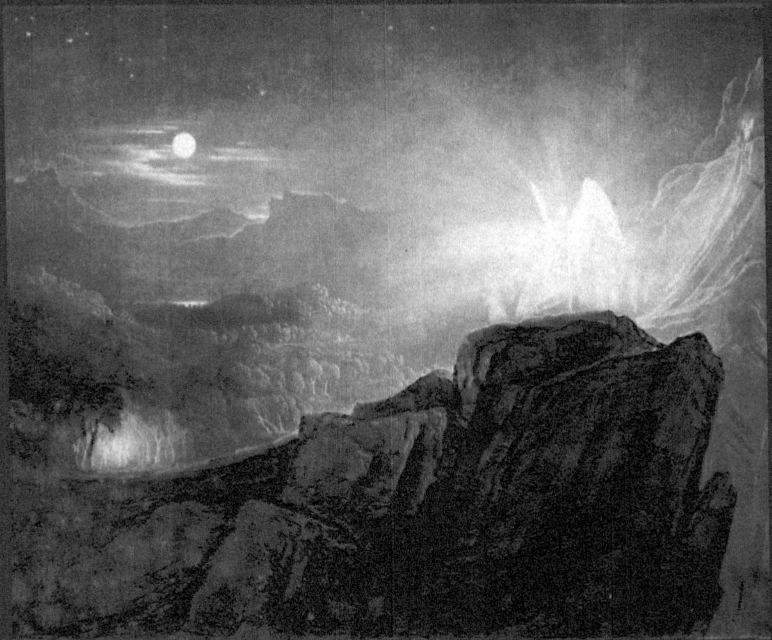

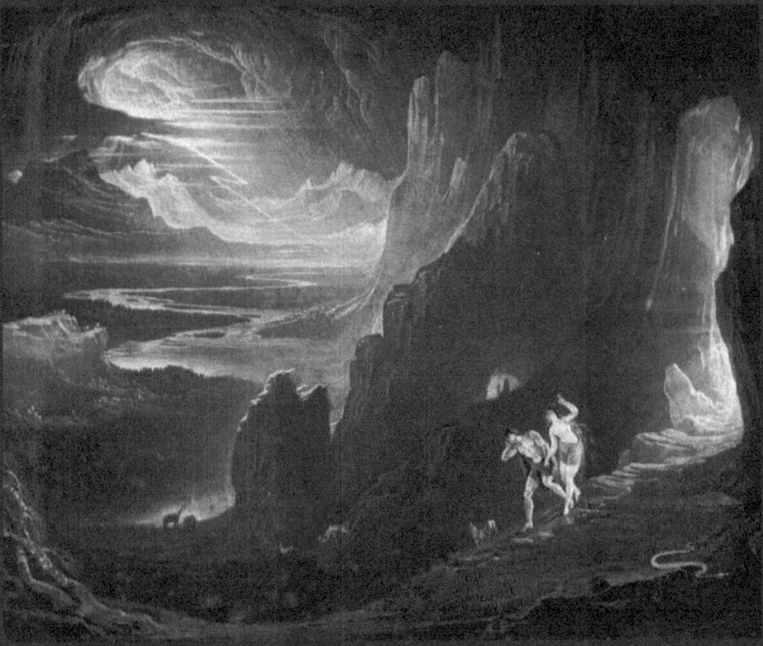

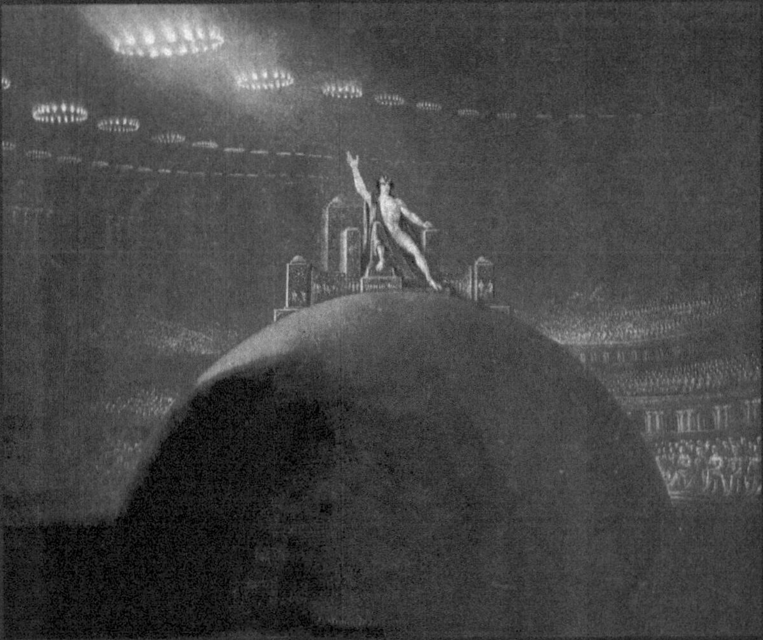

Faith, abuse, t
In the balance with t
The demons you hi

tempered in tl
An iron will consumes
Unrelenting torme

The lure that drew y
We've been blind.
Stripped away

st and misuse,
e chair and the noose.
e have lost control,
flames of hell.
s all, a flawless death.
t, unyielding beast.
u in, a hill of graves.
ve burn, ashless.
a rotting God.

Noli me *tangere*

COLLECTION II

Compendium Of Demonology and Magic

(ca. 1775)

A SELECTION OF PAGES FROM AN EIGHTEENTH-CENTURY DEMONOLOGY BOOK COMPRISED OF MORE THAN THIRTY EXQUISITE WATERCOLOURS SHOWING VARIOUS DEMON FIGURES, AS WELL AS MAGIC AND CABBALISTIC SIGNS. THE FULL LATIN TITLE OF **COMPENDIUM RARISSIMUM TOTIUS ARTIS MAGICAE SISTEMATISATAE PER CELEBERRIMOS ARTIS HUJUS MAGISTROS**, ROUGHLY TRANSLATES TO "A RARE SUMMARY OF THE ENTIRE MAGICAL ART BY THE MOST FAMOUS MASTERS OF THIS ART".

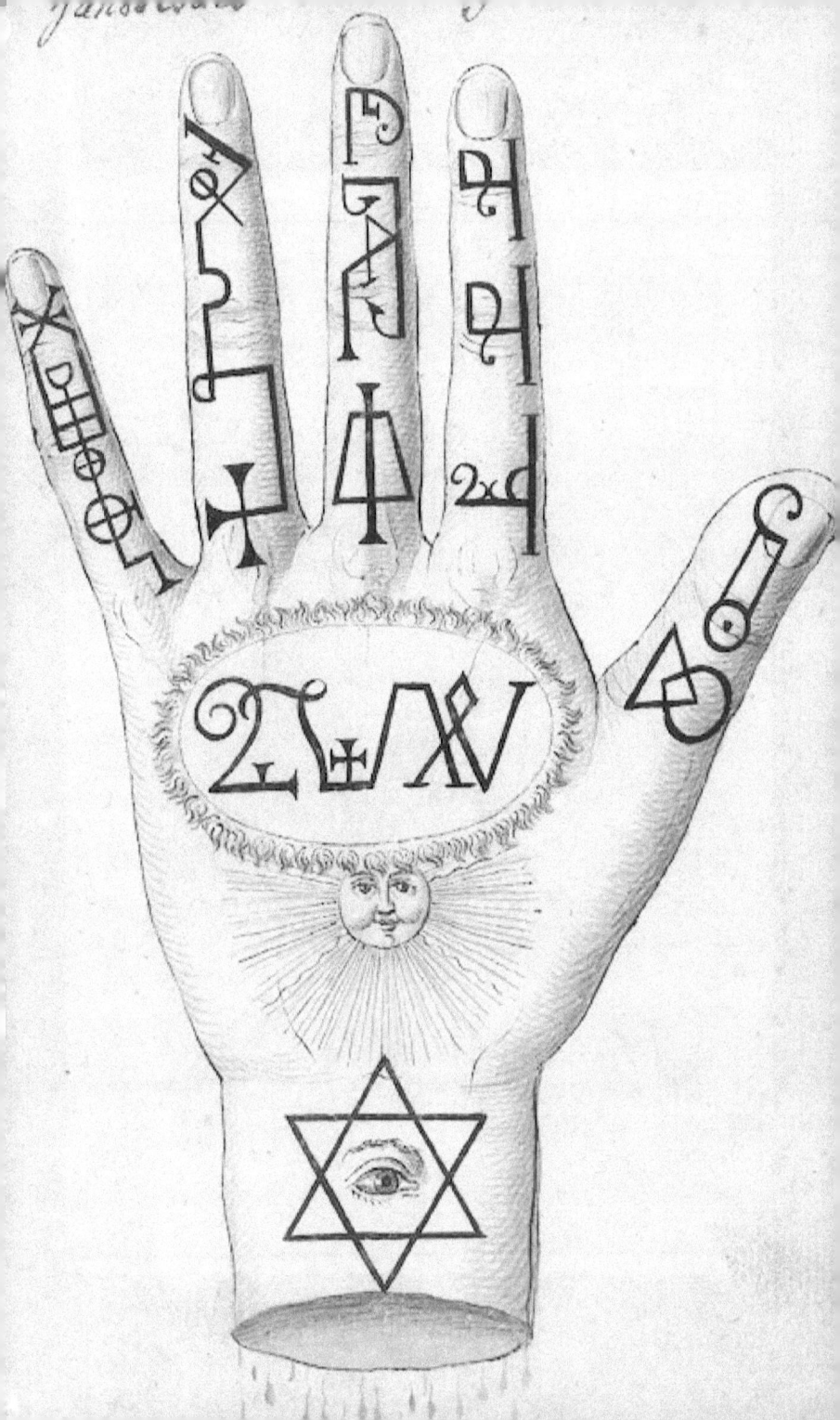

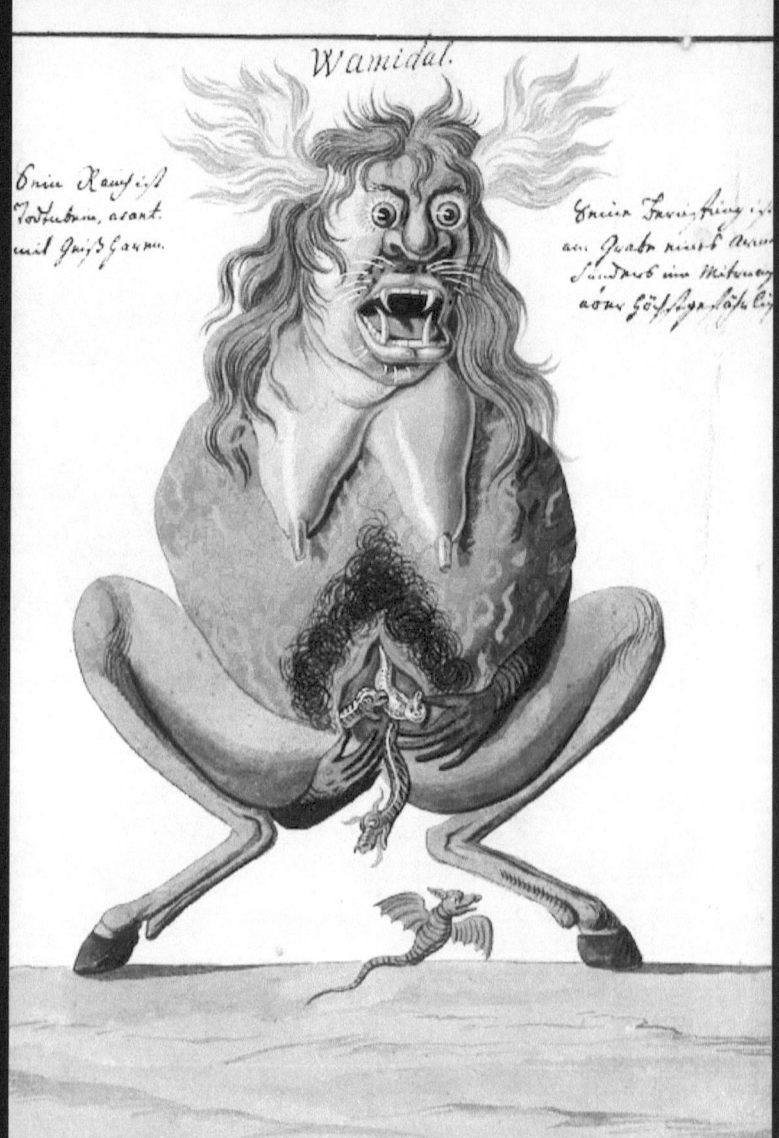

Frevelhaftes Schaz=Graben.
ohne Kanntnis der Operation. d: 1668.
zu N:

Operatio Nigromantica, in qua Princeps Spirituum
Malorum conjurari solet dictus *Astaroth.* Incipit
hora undecima, et durat usq 12 Noctis. Operatio hac
periculosissima est dificile enim est Conjuratum dimittere.

Eine Kauf A. Der fürst der finsternis: Dagol:
Hatn von gefunden
und frisch black.

⚵ ✳ ⊃⊢⊦⊦

FALSE LIGHT

HUMANITY, OUR WROUGHT,
CEASELESS DISEASE.
UNFOLDING MADNESS,
THE EARTH BELOW ME SPEAKS.
SUBTLE NAUSEA,
A CLENCHED FIST WHILE BLIND.
FUCKED BEHIND CAMERA,
HEMORRHAGING INSIDE.
SOAKING UP SHIT BEFORE YOU END.

I'M STILL A FUCKING PARIAH.

THROW AWAY TALENT, TEARS IN THE MATTRESS.

CASH ON THE FLOOR,

BLOOD IN THE HEADDRESS.

BUT THINGS WILL END.

FALSE LIGHT,

THERE'S LESS OF ME THEN THERE WAS BEFORE.

DEATH FUCKING KNOWS YOU,

DEATH FUCKING OWNS YOU.

A ROTTEN WOUND FILLED WITH MAGGOTS.
SCOOP THEM OUT LIKE A CAT'S TONGUE.
BLINDS DRAWN, COVERED IN SHIT.
PAY-PER-VIEW TO MY KINGDOM OF SMUT.

Prey for eyes.
Greener the lawn,
the deeper the grave.

HIDDEN EYES IN THE GARDEN WALLS.
THEY SMELL OUR SULFUR LEAVES.
LIKE DUST IN THESE HALLOWED HALLS.
DARKER THE NIGHT, CLEANER THE KILL.
COARSE LEATHER OF A BUTCHERS GLOVE.
SMOOTH WARMTH OF A JACKAL'S MASK.
I WILL FEED THIS ENDLESS THIRST,
I WILL FEEL MY GOD'S KISS.
I'M PREPPING MY BLADES,
I'M TYING MY KNOTS,

I'm grinding my teeth.

Don't make me wait.

THIS LUST FOR LIFE.
THIS LUST FOR FLESH.
THIS LUST SKIN AND BONE.
THIS LUST FOR DEATH.

CULT-
DE-SAC

COLLECTION III

The Spirit Photographs of William Hope

1905

THE SPIRIT PHOTOGRAPHS OF WILLIAM HOPE

This collection of photographs was unearthed in a Lancashire antiquarian bookshop by one of the curators at the National Media Museum. Known as "spirit photographs", they were taken by a controversial medium called William Hope.

Born in 1863 in Crewe, Hope started his working life as a carpenter, but in 1905 became interested in spirit photography after capturing the supposed image of a ghost while photographing a friend. He went on to found and lead a group of six spirit photographers known as the Crewe Circle. Following World War I, support for the group, and demand for its services, grew as the grieving relatives of those lost to the war sought a means of contacting their loved ones.

By 1922 Hope had moved to London where he established himself as a professional medium. The work of the Crew Circle was investigated on various occasions, the most famous of these taking place in 1922, when the Society for Psychical Research sent Harry Price to investigate. Price collected evidence that Hope was substituting glass plates bearing ghostly images in order to produce his spirit photographs. Later the same year Price published his findings, exposing Hope as a fraudster. However, many of Hope's most ardent supporters spoke out on his behalf, the most famous being Sir Arthur Conan Doyle who wrote The Case for Spirit Photography, in response to Price's claims of fraud. Hope continued to practice, despite his exposure, until his death in 1933.

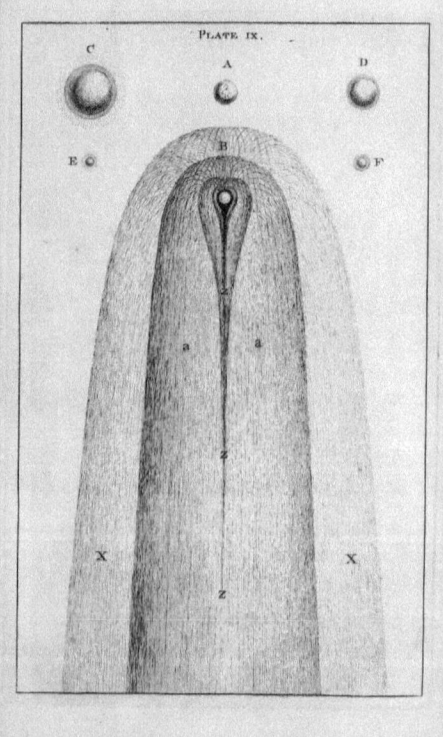

COLLECTION IV

Thomas Wright's An Original Theory or New Hypothesis of the Universe

1750

"I OWN I CAN NEVER LOOK UPON THE STARS WITHOUT WONDERING WHY THE WHOLE WORLD DOES NOT BECOME ASTRONOMERS"

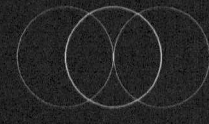

So admits Thomas Wright in An Original Theory or New Hypothesis of the Universe (1750). Written in the form of nine letters to a nameless friend, the book puts forwards "my Theory of the Universe, and the Ideas I have form'd of the known Creation."

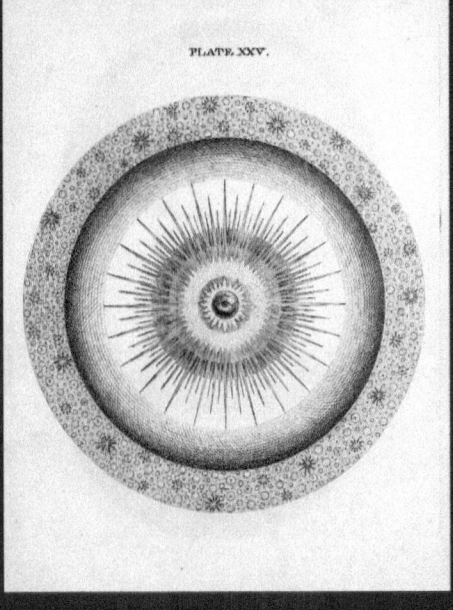

PLATE XXV.

You were born in the Black Fog Mountains. A Miner's son in a godless town. One way in but no way out. Shit kid, you're fucked. Twenty years you've been shoveling shit. *Never asked a Goddamn thing.* Oh baby when you sniff that sludge, it'll bring ya to your fucking knees. We've been fed these *American lies*. Work hard and pray to God. Kneel down, close your eyes.Bleed the cattle, slaughter the lamb. Float me down your river of gold. Sweet venom in my veins, drowning in the words you sold. When I finally washed ashore, I was covered with leper's skin. *No savior on a golden chariot.* No light in the tunnel of death. Persona non grata, bound by a murderers pact. He sold me a way out. I ain't no honest man. The machines came rolling in. Fat man spits lies for profit. *Spoken through broken lungs, hiatal hernias and welfare checks.* Done a job for a city man, running meth through the Cumberland Steppe. It paid well but I lost my mind. Now the mountains crumble like sand. **No honest man.**

Figure du Monstre, q...
Bête est de la taille d'un jeune Taure...
et les Enfans elle boit leur San...
Il est promis 2700th à...

desole le Gévaudan,

lle attaque de préference les Femmes

ur coupe la Tête et l'emporte.

tueraitcet animal

COLLECTION V

The Beast of Gévaudan

1764–1767

In the 1760s, nearly three hundred people were killed in a remote region of south-central France called the Gévaudan (today part of the département of Lozère). The killer was thought to be a huge animal, which came to be known simply as "*the Beast*"; but while the creature's name remained simple, its reputation soon grew extremely complex. Not only was the Beast of Gévaudan said to prefer attacking women and children (and above all small girls), according to firsthand accounts published in the press it often "removed the victim's head and drank all her blood", leaving nothing behind but a pile of bones.

"Reddish brown with dark ridged stripe down the back. Resembles wolf/hyena but big as a donkey. Long gaping jaw, six claws, pointy upright ears and supple furry tail — mobile like a cat's and can knock you over. Cry: more like horse neighing than wolf howling."

Source gallica.bnf.fr / Bibliothèque national

Le 2 May elle dévora cette
Fille au Village de S.t Alban

Le 22 Avril dernier
un jeune 3 Garçon au Village

elle dévora à
la Pergeresse

des ravages affreux causés par la cruelle Bête du Gevaudan, qui continue de désoler ce Pays, malgré
poursuites et recherche continuelle de M.rs Denneval et autres fameux 3 Chasseurs.

A Paris chez Mondhare rue S. Jacques à l'Hôtel Saumur

Abschilderung des, seit dem Monath Sept. des 1764.en Jahrs zu Gevaudan in der Provintz Languedoc in Franckreich, denn
sich zeigenden wilden Thiers Hyene, sonsten Vielfrass genannt.

What the fuck are you looking for in the frozen
midnight sky? Third finger is a sign of strength
and love for human flesh. Blood lust. Barbed
tongue. I can't control my shakes. Red flesh,
burnt hair. Mine are the eyes of the beast.

Wait! I am not what you think.
Unchain me!
Dogs only feed on the vain.
Watch me!

Prey on virgin eyes and sweet auburn curls.
Wait for my scent, you can make it if you run.
Sheltered, satiated, not alone. What am I but a
leper king? Fed through the hate machine.
What am I but a locust dream? Fed through the
hate machine.

HOWLER

PIGS WILL SWING

Weather man sighs in subtle blue.
Rain of lead on a summer night.
Animals through a chlorine bath, cleaned for con-
sumption.

Read 'em and weep, Pigs will swing,
only you and me.

Our forefathers laugh from their tombs.
Traded wounds for a fiscal disease.
Now they sit in their castles abroad.
Kiss their wives and fuck the prom queens.

Weather man cries in a deeper red.
Rain of lead on an autumn night.
We've been cleared for admission through the bar-
rel of a smoking gun.

Only you and me, Pigs will swing.
Read 'em and weep, Pigs will swing.
Tell me all your truths,
only you and me.

Modern man will bleed.

Marc Sergenian
Bass

Wilson Flores

Drums

Chris Marotta

Vocals

Mike Beaujean
Guitar

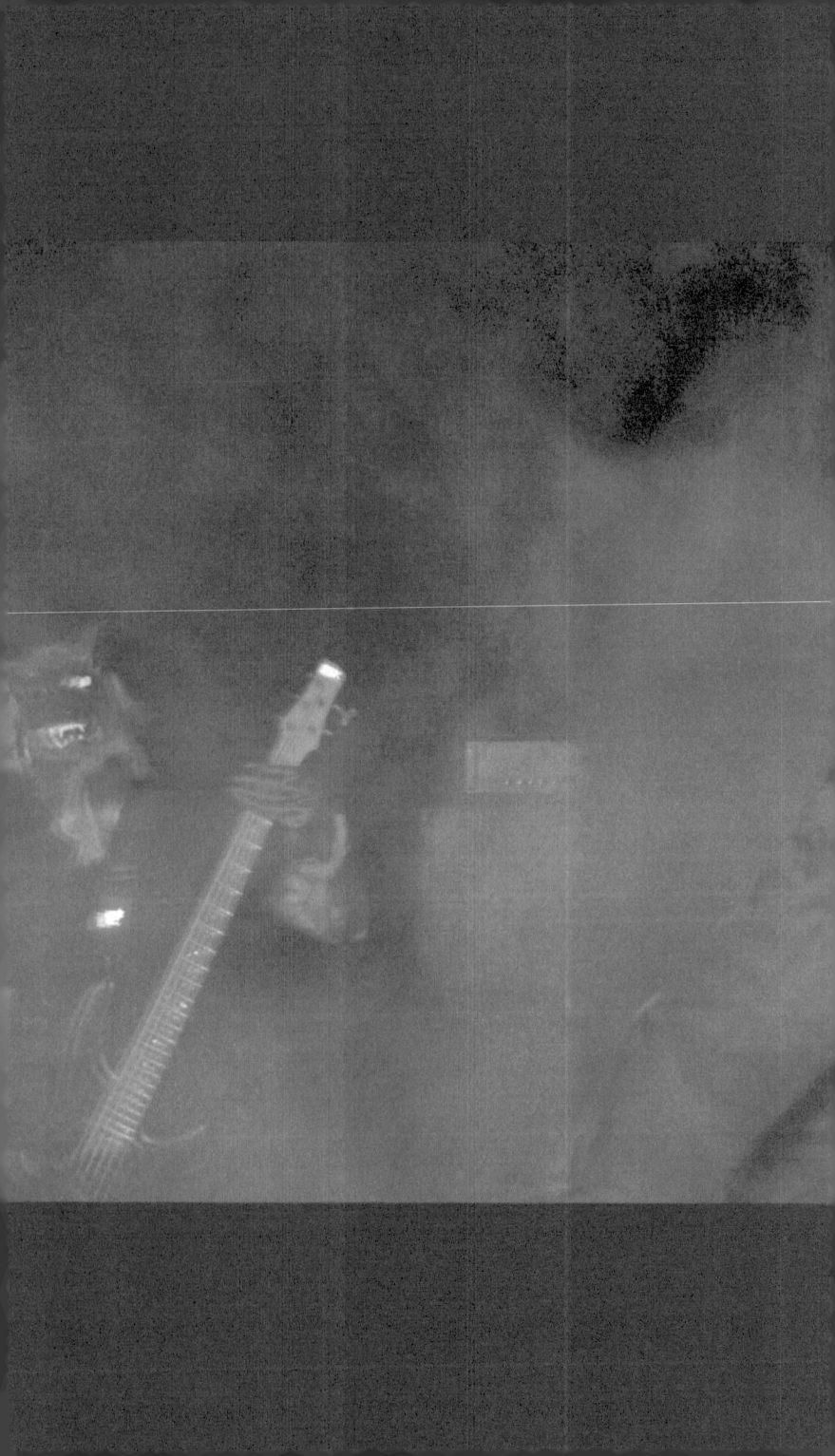

The art of dreams

"Half our dayes wee passe in the shadowe of the earth, and the brother of death exacteth a third part of our lives."

Thomas Browne,
On Dreams

"...night after night, with calm incuriousness we open the door into that ghostly underworld, and hold insane revels with fantastic spectres, weep burning tears for empty griefs, babble with foolish laughter at witless jests, stain our souls with useless crime, or fly with freezing blood from the grasp of an unnamed dread ; and, with the morning, saunter serenely back from these wild adventures into the warm precincts of the cheerful day, unmoved, unstartled, and forgetting."

Elizabeth Bisland
Dreams and their Mysteries

Dreams have long proved a fertile ground for human creativity and expression, and no less so than in the visual arts, giving rise to some of its most arresting images. In addition to the many and varied dreams so important to religion and myth there has emerged, in the last few centuries since the birth of Romanticism, an exploration of the more personal dream-world. Indeed, with its link to the unconscious, the form has perhaps proved the perfect vehicle for those artists looking to surface that which lies submerged - desire, guilt, fear, ambition - to bring to light the truth the waking mind keeps hidden.

No doubt, also, artists have been attracted to the challenge of giving form to something so visually intangible as a dream, a challenge taken up in many ways through the centuries. More often than not there appears the sleeping body itself, with the dream element incorporated in a variety of ways. Common is for the dream sequence to appear in a totally separate part of the image, as if projected on the walls of the sleeping mind: often in the midst of that familiar floating cloud, but also as emerging from nearby objects or events of the day. Also common, particularly in the depiction of nightmares, is for the figures of the dream to simply appear as though in the room with the sleeper, often directly upon the body itself. With the advent of photography, and the potential of double exposures, we see also a different way of trying to capture that intangibility of the dream image. With both the Grandville and Redon images featured, and the work of the Surrealists they anticipate, we see a different approach entirely, one which looks past the sleeper to focus solely on the imagery of the dream itself, and in the process perhaps giving a more true impression of the strangeness and otherworldliness which so often characterises the dream experience.

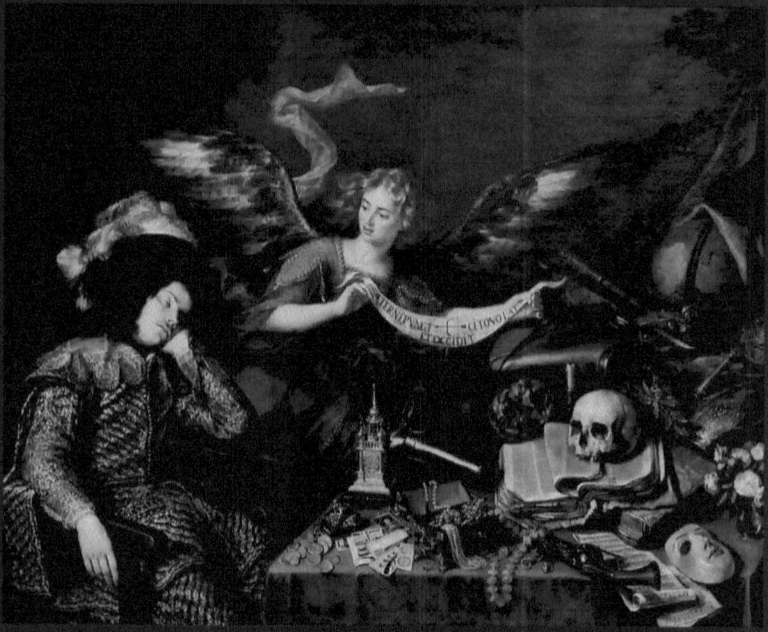

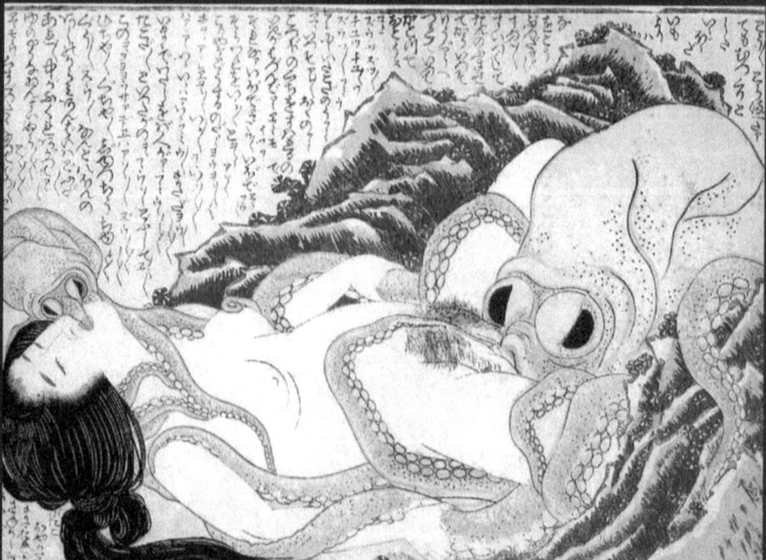

Im 1525 Jar Durch den Pfingstag zwischen der Mittwoch und Pfingstag In der Nacht Im Schlaff hab Ich
das gesicht gesehen wie fil grosser Wasser vom Himel fillen und das erst traff das ertrich Im grosser Weit
Vom Mir. Mit einer solchen grausamkheit mit einem vber grossen rauschen und zersprützen vnd ertrenckht
das ganz Lant. In solchem erschrack Ich so ganz schwärlich das Ich daruon erwachet ehe der ander Wasser fillen
vnd die Wasser die so fillen die Waren sehr vil vnd der ein etlich weit etlich nächer das zu komen so fiel Sinck das
Ich gedanckht sich langsam fiel. aber da das erst Wasser das ertrich pracht naher ffie Seiher kam so fiel es mit einer
solchen geschwindikheit wint vnd Brausen das Ich als so erschrack da Ich erwacht das mir alle mein Leichnam
zittert vnd Lang weit nicht zu mir selber kam. aber da Ich am morgens auff stund Mallet Ich hie oben Wie Ichs
gesehen hatte. Got werde alles ding zum besten.

                                                      Albrecht Dürer

COCHEMARE

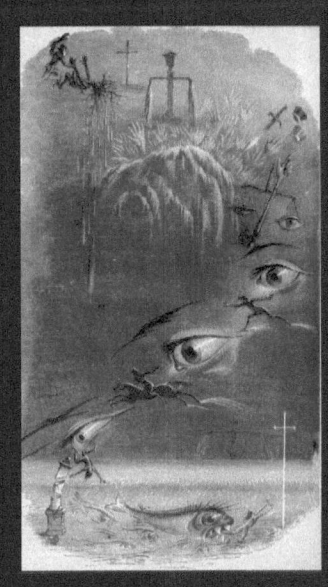

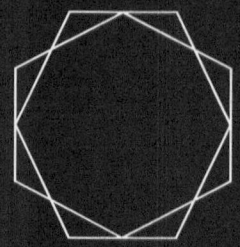

I Was The Whirlwind, The
Tempest Of Fire, Bleeding
Flames Into The Air.
But Of Course
We're All A Lie.

YOU CAME TO ME AGAIN. A LITTLE VOICE INSIDE MY HEAD. WE ALL BLEED LIKE THE FIRST MEN. SMILE BABY, THE INFECTION'S SPREAD.

I fought for as long as I could. I caught your gaze of torment. I fell in love with your venom eyes, I fell in love with your venom.
A lying tongue, sharp as a sword. Crack of thunder, a mouth for war.
I shed my armor, made of glass. A sudden breadth in the black mass.
You took your time, swallowed me whole.
I fought for as long as I could. I caught your gaze of torment. I fell in love with your venom eyes, I fell in love with your venom.
A lying tongue, sharp as a sword.
Crack of thunder, a mouth for war.
I shed my armor, made of glass.
A sudden breadth in the black mass.

You took your time, swallowed me whole.

BOW DOWN, KING OF SILK ON A THRONE OF STILTS.

Bow down, king of silk on a throne of stilts. Bow your head, hail to the weak. Married into the hate. You were always the imposter king. Boy was weak and an easy kill.

Weak lies through feeble lips, never spit the truth. Fetishize those golden gates. Maybe once you had a chance. Tried to buy their loyalty. Just bloody and weak.

In their eyes are only worms. In their hearts is only salt.In their minds I'm only one. In her eyes I'm only one. Only one. Hey kid, take a look at us now, corpses rolling through the sands of time.

Nine times out of ten, we were beat, bloodied and broken.

But you never really lost your way.
Serpent's tongue was always there.
Choke us all to keep the smile. Feed the snake it's poison.

Skin pulled tight like a canvas.
Cut the rot and lie in silence.
Edge of death is meaningless.

Save the man but leave the disease.
They saved the man but left the disease.
They saved the man but left the disease.
You met the reaper, It was always me.

VOIDWALKER

All dead do a hollow dance, lecherous and stubborn. A Grim waltz in 3/4 time. Deaf and defeated. To the chatter of a loosened jaw, milk the tit of your southern god.

Break your chains; beat them to the swords. Crush 'em all or serve your time. A thousand years in the void. All men are slaves to their eyes, unseen and unworthy.

Cold hands, reaching for your neck. Damned and deleted, tear down the walls bought with your blood.

Master of the earth, long have I waited, long have you learned. Drag them down but keep them alive.

Phosphene Dream

PRISONER'S CINEMA

They came in the black of night,
dancers on the edge of oblivion.
That oh so subtle light, my
eyes a sweet meridian. A riot
in no common tongue, born in
darkness and nurtured by lust.
Only silence fills your lungs.
Only blood, dust & guts. Eyes
open or closed? hands bloodied
or clean? Darkness has become
my stage, a warm phosphene
dream. Sleep or Sleep Walker,
they dance in your Mother's
gown. How the hell did we get
here? I wear a fragile crown.
The Architect, The Mason.
I built these prison walls, I
swallowed the key. The Warden,
The Executioner. Lines dance
in the darkness. Poisoned
walls speak to me. Eyes open
or closed? Hands bloodied or
clean? Darkness has become
my stage, A warm phosphene
dream. Frozen stiff or burned
alive. Defiled and dethroned.
We were born with silver horns.
Your fear is all I've known. Cold
american death.

☐ **DESCENDER by Descender** (ALR 001)
6 song debut EP. Available formats: Digipak CD, digital / streaming
90's Influenced post-hardcore. RIYL: Snapcase, Helmet, Quicksand

"Angularly aggressive hardcore that takes an abrasive shape on purpose." – CMJ

☐ **AND SO WE MARCHED by Descender** (ALR 002)
4 song EP. Available formats: Printed book, digital / streaming
90's Influenced post-hardcore. RIYL: Snapcase, Helmet, Quicksand

*"...a 21st Century compliant post-hardcore band that was raised on metal and got
dosed with a tab of AmRep..."* – Jaded Scenster

☐ **TAKING DRUGS TO MAKE MUSIC TO SELL CARS TO
by Human Highlight Reel** (ALR 003)
4 song debut EP. Available formats: Vinyl record, printed book, digital / streaming
Instrumental post-rock. RIYL: Maserati, June of 44, Russian Circles

"Aces instrumental post rock. Think Russian Circles or perhaps a more metal Seam..."
– Jaded Scenster

☐ **JUDGE by Vagina Panther** (ALR 004)
5 song EP. Available formats: Printed book, digital / streaming
Heavy female-fronted garage rock. RIYL: QOTSA, Cheeseburger, Fu Manchu, Stooges

"Vagina Panther rocks." – Billboard

☐ **BLACK BLACK BLACK by Black Black Black** (ALR 005)
12 song debut LP. Available formats: Vinyl record, printed book, digital / streaming
Melodic death rock. RIYL: Akimbo, Torche, Lungfish, Black Flag

*"Brooklyn-by-way-of-Ohio doomsters offer up a big, nasty salute to gas tanks and goat
hooves. It all coalesces to form one ravaging feast of melodic death rock that will satiate
all your salacious needs, be it Nether-deity worshiping or rock star living."* – Broken Beard

☐ **GODMAKER by Godmaker** (ALR 007)
4 song debut LP. Available formats: Vinyl record, printed book, digital / streaming
Doomy sludge metal. RIYL: High on Fire, Red Fang, Mastodon, The Sword

*"An example of genuine out-of-nowhere brilliance. A patient drawn out campaign
of aggression."* – Relix

☐ **THE SPACE MERCHANTS by The Space Merchants** (ALR 008)
8 song debut LP. Available formats: Printed book, digital / streaming
Whiskey-soaked space-rock. RIYL: Black Mountain, Dead Meadow, The Besnard Lakes

*"A unique brand of lo-fi psych rock... their huge-yet-minimal sound, mixing psych with
blues and country style riffs to make something great."* – Magnet

☐ **HIRAM-MAXIM by Hiram-Maxim** (ALR 009)
4 song debut LP. Available formats: Vinyl record, printed book, digital / streaming
Noisy experimental doomgaze. RIYL: Swans, Suicide, Pink Floyd, Oxbow

*"Builds into an apocalyptic fervor before dissipating into a cloudy haze & ending before
you've had your fill."* – VICE

☐ **ALTERED STATES OF DEATH AND GRACE by Black Black Black** (ALR 010)
10 song sophomore LP. Available formats: Vinyl record, printed book, digital / streaming
Melodic death rock. RIYL: Akimbo, Torche, Lungfish, Black Flag

*"...the kind of good-natured misanthropy of bands like Whores or KEN mode, but the musical
gestures beneath the noisy exterior are all forward-charging, Kyuss-worshipping sludge n' roll.
It's basically underground metal's version of a radio banger."* – BrooklynVegan

☐ **TRESPASSES by Nathaniel Shannon & The Vanishing Twin** (ALR 011)
15 song debut LP. Available formats: Printed book, digital / streaming
Unsettling bedroom recording darkness. RIYL: Lanegan, Badalemnti, Springsteen, Waits

*"An unsettling yet captivating collection of songs compiled from a decade of bedroom
recordings... Shannon's spoken word-style vocals over haunting and minimalist
instrumentals lend a creepy atmosphere to the record."* – Decibel

☐ FERA by Husbandry (ALR 012)

8 song debut LP. Available formats: Printed book, CD, digital / streaming
Female-fronted math rock meets post-hardcore. RIYL: Mars Volta, Glassjaw, Refused, Deftones

"It's hard to believe that Husbandry is not the biggest band in the world. They're heavy and mathy, chaos wrapped in hard rock and heavy metal." – Nerdist

☐ MURDEREDMAN by MURDEREDMAN (ALR 013)

8 song sophomore LP. Available formats: Vinyl record, printed book, digital / streaming
Post-punk inspired noise rock. RIYL: Savages, Bauhaus, Boris, Killing Joke

"A patient and disciplined examination of anxiety and melancholy underpinned with a cathartic tension-and-release structure that borrows from goth, post-metal, and no-wave..." – New Noise Magazine

☐ IN TENSIONS by Lo-Pan (ALR 014)

5 song EP. Available formats: Vinyl record, printed book, CD, digital / streaming
Anthemic desert rock. RIYL: Soundgarden, ASG, Torche, Red Fang

"Calling Lo-Pan a stoner band is a disservice to the amalgam of influences the band successfully merges together: the soulful alt rock of the 90s with a thundering doom/sludge sound that's equal parts immediate and timeless." – Nine Circles

☐ GHOSTS by Hiram-Maxim (ALR 015)

7 song LP. Available formats. Vinyl record, printed book, digital / streaming
Noisy experimental doomgaze. RIYL: Swans, Suicide, Pink Floyd, Oxbow

"Everything is awash in mesmerizing ambient skree and squalls of atonal feedback. Think an extended, updated version of side 2 of Black Flag's My War." – Hellride Music

☐ KISS THE DIRT by The Space Merchants (ALR 016)

10 song sophomore LP. Available formats: Vinyl record, printed book, digital / streaming
Whiskey-soaked space-rock. RIYL: Black Mountain, Dead Meadow, The Besnard Lakes

"[T]he sonic equivalent of having an acid trip in the bathroom between Woodstock and a ZZ Top concert in '69" – New Noise Magazine

☐ BAD WEEDS NEVER DIE by Husbandry (ALR 017)

5 song EP. Available formats: Printed book, CD, digital / streaming
Female-fronted math rock meets post-hardcore. RIYL: Mars Volta, Glassjaw, Refused, Deftones

"While retaining their bold go-anywhere style, the EP is a more streamlined and focused effort, signaling a greater maturity and command of recording." – Echoes and Dust

☐ BY THE GRACE OF BLOOD AND GUTS by Haan (ALR 018)

8 song LP. Available formats: Printed book, Vinyl, CD, digital / streaming
Noise, Grime, Sludge, Metal, Rock. RIYL: Unsane, Melvins, Swans, Helmet, Clutch

"If Melvins and Unsane had a kid while under the influence of hallucinogens" – Metal Insider

☐ LUMINOUS VOLUMES by Skryptor (ALR 019)

7 song LP. Available formats: Vinyl, Printed book, CD, digital / streaming
Noise, Math rock, Prog. RIYL: craw, Dazzling Killmen, Don Cabellero

"Galloping, off-kilter and unabashedly victorious, proggy noise-rock outfit Skryptor's takes hard-rock/psychedelic throwback tropes, flips them on their heads and stretches it all into an adventurous march through endlessly shifting soundscapes."" – Revolver

☐ DEAD INSIDE by Frayle (ALR 021)

7 song 7". Alchemy Box: Printed book, Vinyl, CD, digital / streaming
Heavy witch doom. RIYL: Chelsea Wolfe, Portis Head, Sleep, Sunn O)))

"Trades in dark psychedelics and heavy, dripping drums that punctuate the riffing that plays in and around vocalist Gywn Strang's superb voice." – Nine Circles

☐ SUBTLE by Lo-Pan (ALR 022)

11 song LP. Available formats: Vinyl, Printed book, CD, digital / streaming
Anthemic desert rock. RIYL: Soundgarden, ASG, Torche, Red Fang

Subtle was produced by James Brown (NIN, Foo Fighters, Ghost) and mastered by Ted Jensen (Mastodon, Deftones, Bad Company, GNR).

☐ **1692** by Frayle (ALR 023)
8 song LP. Available formats: Vinyl, Printed book, CD, digital / streaming
Heavy witch doom. RIYL: Chelsea Wolfe, Portishead, Sleep

"Haunting, hypnotic mix of crushing Sleep-style doom and cooing ethereal vocals à la Cocteau Twins'
Elizabeth Fraser." – Revolver

☐ **DESTROYER DELIVER** by Zeb Gould (ALR 024)
8 song LP. Available formats: Printed book, CD, digital / streaming
Indie-style gloom-folk meets fingerpicking prairie-bliss. RIYL: Neil Young, Gillian Welch, Bill Callahan
A post-Millenium take on melancholic wasteland love.

☐ **THE THREE MOTHERS** by Nathaniel Shannon & the Vanishing Twin (ALR 025)
3 song EP. Available formats: Limited Edition Cassette Box, digital / streaming
THE THREE MOTHERS is a primordial fixation with Dario Argento's trilogy's witches. RIYL: Lanegan,
Badalemnti, Springsteen, Tom Waits

"There are very few times that you listen to music and it's something brand new. Something that has
it's own identity and style. Nathaniel Shannon's new EP delivers a passionate dark dreamscape of life.
His leathery dark vocals are ominous as the music that he creates. Close your eyes and you're suddenly
walking down a street with faceless people and distant sound of sirens." – Steve Austin (Today is the Day
/ Austin Enterprises)

☐ **PRISONER'S CINEMA** by Burning Tongue (ALR 026)
11 song LP. Available formats: Vinyl, Printed book, CD, digital / streaming
Crushing nihilism that nod to the shadowy side of hardcore punk. RIYL: Power Trip, Craft, G.I.S.M.

With chainsaw guitars, pummeling double-bass and a barking prophet preaching an end times message,
Burning Tongue is here to remind you that the plague has arrived and rain piss all over your pitiful
socially-distanced BBQs, park hangs and elbow daps.

☐ **THE LINE, ITS WIDTH, AND THE WARDRONE** by Rebreather (ALR 028)
11 song LP. Available formats: Vinyl, Printed book, CD, digital / streaming
Doom, Sludge, Metal, Prog. RIYL Part Chimp,Unsane, Melvins.

Rebreather creates punishing, and teneacious music that seethes and breathes.

☐ **SKIN & SORROW** by Frayle (ALR 033)
11 song LP. Available formats: Vinyl, Printed book, CD, digital / streaming
Heavy, Witch, Doom. Haunting, hypnotic mix of crushing Sleep-style doom and cooing ethereal vocals à la
Cocteau Twins' Elizabeth Fraser.

☐ **THUNDERHEADS** by LaMACCHIA (ALR 034)
11 song LP. Available formats: Vinyl, Printed book, CD, digital / streaming
Egnimatic layered & moody Rock. RIYL: Liars, Doves, Autolux, Radiohead. Debut by guitarist & vocalist
John LaMacchia from Candiria).

JOIN THE AQUALAMB RESEARCH CLUB

Your role in Aqualamb Research Club is simple. All we want is to hear from you—what you like, what
you hate, and why. A year of Aqualamb Research Club will cost you 10 bucks, which just about
covers packaging and mailing. In return, you will get a lot of fine music, an Aqualamb T-shirt, and
a special Aqualamb Research Club pin plus the chance to influence the course of music.

No strings, no gimmicks, no dumb offers or obligations. We just want to tune in to your taste.

EMAIL INFO@AQUALAMB.ORG FOR MORE INFO ON HOW YOU CAN BE A PART OF OUR RESEARCH.

Aqualamb

The music for *Prisoner's Cinema*
can be downloaded via the link below:

aqualamb.org/026

www.ingramcontent.com/pod-product-compliance
Lightning Source LLC
Chambersburg PA
CBHW050904180626
46814CB00007B/2884